Four Caribbean Folk Tales

THE ILLUSTRATED
ANANSI

Philip Sherlock

Illustrated by
Petrina Wright

CARIBBEAN

First published 1995 by
MACMILLAN EDUCATION LTD
London and Basingstoke
Companies and representatives throughout the world

ISBN 0–333–63120–X

12	11	10	9	8	7	6	5	4	3
06	05	04	03	02	01	00	99	98	97

This book is printed on paper suitable for recycling and
made from fully managed and sustained forest sources.

Printed in Hong Kong

A catalogue record for this book is available from the
British Library.

CONTENTS

From Tiger to Anansi   4

Anansi and Turtle and Pigeon   18

The Quarrel   24

Anansi and the Crabs   36

From Tiger
to Anansi

Once upon a time and a long long time ago the Tiger was king of the forest.

At evening when all the animals sat together in a circle and talked and laughed together, Snake would ask:

'Who is the strongest of us all?'

'Tiger is strongest,' cried Dog. 'When Tiger whispers the trees listen. When Tiger is angry and cries out, the trees tremble.'

'And who is the weakest of all?' asked Snake.

'Anansi,' shouted Dog, and they all laughed together. 'Anansi the spider is weakest of all. When he whispers no one listens. When he shouts everyone laughs.'

Now one day the weakest and the strongest came face to face, Anansi and Tiger. They met in a clearing of the forest. The frogs hiding under the cool leaves saw them. The bright–green parrots in the branches heard them.

When they met, Anansi bowed so low that his forehead touched the ground. Tiger did not greet him. Tiger just looked at Anansi.

'Good morning, Tiger, ' cried Anansi. ' I have a favour to ask.'

'And what is it, Anansi?' said Tiger.

'Tiger, we all know that you are strongest of us all. This is why we give your name to many things. We have Tiger lilies and Tiger stories and Tiger moths, and Tiger this and Tiger that. Everyone knows that I am weakest of all. This is why nothing bears my name. Tiger, let something be called after the weakest one so that men may know my name too.'

'Well,' said Tiger, without so much as a glance toward Anansi, 'what would you like to bear your name?'

'The stories,' cried Anansi. 'The stories that we tell in the forest at evening time when the sun goes down, the stories about Br'er Snake and Br'er Tacumah, Br'er Cow and Br'er Bird and all of us.'

Now Tiger liked these stories and he meant to keep them as Tiger stories. He thought to himself, How stupid, how weak this Anansi is. I will play a trick on him so that all the animals will laugh at him. Tiger moved his tail slowly from side to side and said, 'Very good, Anansi, very good. I will let the stories be named after you, if you do what I ask.'

'Tiger, I will do what you ask.'

'Yes, I am sure you will, I am sure you will,' said Tiger, moving his tail slowly from side to side. 'It is a little thing that I ask. Bring me Mr. Snake alive. Do you know Snake who lives down by the river, Mr. Anansi? Bring him to me alive and you can have the stories.'

Tiger stopped speaking. He did not move his tail. He looked at Anansi and waited for him to speak. All the animals in the forest waited. Mr. Frog beneath the cool leaves, Mr. Parrot up in the tree, all watched Anansi. They were all ready to laugh at him.

'Tiger, I will do what you ask,' said Anansi. At these words a great wave of laughter burst from the forest. The frogs and parrots laughed. Tiger laughed loudest of all, for how could feeble Anansi catch Snake alive?

Anansi went away. He heard the forest laughing at him from every side.

That was on Monday morning. Anansi sat before his house and thought of plan after plan. At last he hit upon one that could not fail. He would build a Calaban.

On Tuesday morning Anansi built a Calaban. He took a strong vine and made a noose. He hid the vine in the grass. Inside the noose he set some of the berries that Snake loved best. Then he waited. Soon Snake came up the path. He saw the berries and went toward them. He lay across the vine and ate the berries. Anansi pulled at the vine to tighten the noose, but Snake's body was too heavy. Anansi saw that the Calaban had failed.

Wednesday came. Anansi made a deep hole in the ground. He made the sides slippery with grease. In the bottom he put some of the bananas that Snake loved. Then he hid in the bush beside the road and waited.

9

Snake came crawling down the path toward the river. He was hungry and thirsty. He saw the bananas at the bottom of the hole. He saw that the sides of the hole were slippery. First he wrapped his tail tightly round the trunk of a tree, then he reached down into the hole and ate the bananas. When he was finished he pulled himself up by his tail and crawled away. Anansi had lost his bananas and he had lost Snake, too.

Thursday morning came. Anansi made a Fly Up. Inside the trap he put an egg. Snake came down the path. He was happy this morning, so happy that he lifted his head and a third of his long body from the ground. He just lowered his head, took up the egg in his mouth, and never even touched the trap. The Fly Up could not catch Snake.

What was Anansi to do? Friday morning came. He sat and thought all day. It was no use.

Now it was Saturday morning. This was the last day. Anansi went for a walk down by the river. He passed by the hole where Snake lived. There was Snake, his body hidden in the hole, his head resting on the ground at the entrance to the hole. It was early morning. Snake was watching the sun rise above the mountains.

11

'Good morning, Anansi, ' said Snake.

'Good morning, Snake,' said Anansi.

'Anansi, I am very angry with you. You have been trying to catch me all week. You set a Fly Up to catch me. The day before you made a Slippery Hole for me. The day before that you made a Calaban. I have a good mind to kill you, Anansi.'

'Ah, you are too clever, Snake,' said Anansi. 'You are much too clever. Yes, what you say is so. I tried to catch you, but I failed. Now I can never prove that you are the longest animal in the world, longer even than the bamboo tree.'

'Of course I am the longest of all animals,' cried Snake. 'I am much longer than the bamboo tree.'

'What, longer than that bamboo tree across there?' asked Anansi.

'Of course I am,' said Snake. 'Look and see.' Snake came out of the hole and stretched himself out at full length.

'Yes, you are very, very long,' said Anansi, 'but the bamboo tree is very long, too. Now that I look at you and at the bamboo tree I must say that the bamboo tree seems longer. But it's hard to say because it is further away.'

'Well, bring it nearer,' cried Snake. 'Cut it down and put it beside me. You will soon see that I am much longer.'

Anansi ran to the bamboo tree and cut it down. He placed it on the ground and cut off all its branches. Bush, bush, bush, bush! There it was, long and straight as a flagstaff.

'Now put it beside me,' said Snake.

Anansi put the long bamboo tree down on the ground beside Snake. Then he said:

'Snake, when I go up to see where your head is, you will crawl up. When I go down to see where your tail is, you will crawl down. In that way you will always seem to be longer than the bamboo tree, which really is longer than you are.'

'Tie my tail, then!' said Snake. 'Tie my tail! I know that I am longer than the bamboo, whatever you say.'

Anansi tied Snake's tail to the end of the bamboo. Then he ran up to the other end.

'Stretch, Snake, stretch, and we will see who is longer.'

A crowd of animals were gathering round. Here was something better than a race. 'Stretch, Snake, stretch,' they called.

Snake stretched as hard as he could. Anansi tied him round his middle so that he should not slip back. Now one more try. Snake knew that if he stretched hard enough he would prove to be longer than the bamboo.

Anansi ran up to him. 'Rest yourself for a little, Snake, and then stretch again. If you can stretch another six inches you will be longer than the bamboo. Try your hardest. Stretch so that you even have to shut your eyes. Ready?'

'Yes,' said Snake. Then Snake made a mighty effort. He stretched so hard that he had to squeeze his eyes shut.

'Hooray!' cried the animals. 'You are winning, Snake. Just two inches more.'

And at that moment Anansi tied Snake's head to the bamboo. There he was. At last he had caught Snake, all by himself.

The animals fell silent. Yes, there Snake was, all tied up, ready to be taken to Tiger. And feeble Anansi had done this. They could laugh at him no more.

And never again did Tiger dare to call these stories by his name. They were Anansi stories for ever after, from that day to this.

Anansi and Turtle and Pigeon

Turtle once lived next door to Pigeon, and across the road was Anansi's house. Sometimes Turtle and Anansi would stand together and watch Pigeon flying from one house-top to another, from one tree to another.

'I wish I could fly with Pigeon,' said Turtle.

'I wish so, too,' said Anansi.

At last one day they went to Pigeon and asked him to teach them to fly. Pigeon took them to the oldest pigeon of all. He looked as wise as an owl and said that they could learn. Then each pigeon pulled out a feather and glued it to Turtle's back until he looked like a pincushion, all full of feathers. Anansi, they said, would have to let Turtle try first. Next they took hold of Turtle and flew up into the air.

Soon they reached Tiger's cornfield. Every day the pigeons went there and took Tiger's corn. When they got there they took their feathers away from Turtle, gave him a large bag, and told him to pick up the grains of corn from the ground. So they all picked up corn; and Turtle picked up corn, too.

Then they heard a noise.

The pigeons all stood still and lifted up their heads. A second or two later the oldest pigeon flapped his wings and rose up, and all the other pigeons flapped their wings and flew away, leaving Turtle all by himself in the field of corn. Anansi saw the pigeons return home, but there was no Turtle with them. Turtle was left in the middle of the field, and there the watchman found him with the bag of corn.

'So it's you, Turtle, is it? You are the thief that comes and steals Tiger's corn?'

'No,' cried Turtle, 'no, my sweet watchman. Ask Anansi if you doubt me. It is the pigeons that come stealing the corn.'

'What are you doing here, then?' asked the watchman.

'Oh, my sweet watchman,' cried Turtle, 'ask Anansi if you doubt me. I told the pigeons that I wanted to fly, and they lent me feathers and I came with them; but I am not stealing the corn.'

'Well,' said the watchman, 'I never yet saw a turtle fly. You must come with me.' And he put Turtle in a pail of water and took him to Tiger's house.

Now Turtle remembered what Anansi had once told him. Anansi once said: 'Turtle, when you don't know what to say and when you don't know what to do – sing!' So Turtle began to sing. He sang so sweetly that the watchman began to dance, and he danced until he had spilled all the water out of the pail. Then Turtle called out, 'If you let me walk I will sing so sweetly!'

But the watchman said no.

At last they came to Tiger's house, and Tiger came out to see Turtle.

'Ah,' said Tiger, 'call the cook!' Tiger told the cook how to stew Turtle for supper, and then he went off to invite his relations and friends to come to the meal.

Now the cook was mixing all the onions and pimento together, and Turtle remembered what Anansi had said, and Turtle began to sing. He sang so sweetly that the cook began to dance.

Then Turtle said, 'My sweet cook, if you will only put me on the ground outside I will sing so sweetly!'

The cook put Turtle outside, and he sang more sweetly than ever; and the cook danced all the time.

Then Turtle said: 'Oh, my sweet cook, if you will take me to the river and put just the tip of my tail in the water I will sing more sweetly than ever.'

The cook took Turtle to the river and put just the tip of his tail in the water, and Turtle sang more sweetly than ever, and the cook danced and danced.

But soon he heard no singing. He looked down.

There was Turtle at the bottom of the river! And Turtle waved his hand and swam away.

And the cook dared not go back to Tiger's house.

That is why, from that day to this, no one cooks Tiger's food for him.

23

The Quarrel

In the beginning Anansi, Tiger and Monkey were friends. They rented some land down by the river and set about clearing it. Every morning they went off to work, talking and laughing. Anansi talked more than the others. He carried the lunch-box. He liked his lunch very much indeed.

Here was the field. Monkey and Tiger set to work at once. Anansi rested in the shade of the mango tree for a while. Then he went out and worked with his friends for a little. Then he went back to the shade of the tree to see that the lunch was safe. Then he worked a little more. Then he rested a little more. When lunch-time came Tiger and Monkey were very tired, but Anansi was very fresh.

When the field had been cleared, the friends planted Indian corn in it. In the mornings they would go out to see how the young plants were growing. The plants grew quickly and soon began to bear corn. Before long the corn in the ears was full. It was time to reap the corn.

One morning Monkey, Tiger and Anansi were in the field looking at the fine crop of corn. Suddenly Monkey called out. 'Look,' he cried, 'look there! Someone has been breaking the corn. Someone has been stealing our corn!'

Tiger and Anansi looked. It was true. The corn had been reaped in one part of the field. How angry they were! Anansi seemed the angriest of all. He seemed to be so angry that Monkey began to wonder. He knew Anansi well. Could it be that Anansi himself had taken the corn?

Monkey told Tiger what he thought. They decided to watch the field without telling Anansi.

When night came, Monkey and Tiger went to the field. Monkey climbed the mango tree and sat out on a branch. Tiger sat by the fence and watched. There was a full moon, so both Tiger and Monkey could easily see what was happening.

One hour passed, and then another. All was quiet. This is very dull, thought Tiger.

Another hour passed. It was twelve o'clock. Time for bed, said Monkey to himself, rubbing his eyes.

What was that? Down by the southern fence something was moving. There was no wind, but in that part of the field the leaves were bending as if a wind were blowing over them.

Monkey looked carefully. He was quite sure that someone was there. He decided to climb down from the tree quietly, warn Tiger, and then catch the thief.

27

Monkey jumped down from the branch to the ground. It was an easy jump for him, and no one would have heard him if he had not jumped on to a dry stick that lay on the ground. It broke with a noise like a pistol shot. The noise frightened the thief. Both Monkey and Tiger heard the sound of running feet and they followed as quickly as they could. Out of the field they ran, then across the road and in among the trees. The sound of footsteps became clearer. They were gaining on the thief. Now they could see him as he ran across a stretch of open ground. It was Anansi.

Monkey and Tiger were very angry. They ran all the more quickly. Anansi could see that they would soon catch up with him. Besides, he was already growing tired.

Suddenly Anansi saw a grain of corn on the path. 'Help me,' he cried. 'Hide me, hide me, grain of corn.'

The grain of corn opened and closed again. There was Anansi hidden inside the grain of corn. Monkey and Tiger ran past. They did not see the grain of corn. They could not find Anansi.

29

Before long it was morning. As the sun rose, Mr. Rooster flew down from his perch and set off down the path to the river. He was hungry and thirsty. Ah, there on the path in front of him was a grain of corn. He swallowed it quickly. There was Anansi inside the grain of corn inside Mr. Rooster.

Mr. Rooster stood by the bank of the river. He did not see someone who was very hungry. He did not see Mr. Alligator until it was too late. And now there was Mr. Anansi inside Mr. Rooster inside Mr. Alligator.

All this time Monkey and Tiger were looking for Anansi. They looked here, they looked there, but they could not find him.

'I tell you what we will do,' said Monkey at last. 'We'll ask our oracle drum.'

'Yes, the oracle drum will tell us if we beat it in the right way,' said Tiger.

31

Monkey and Tiger placed the oracle drum carefully on the ground. They stood, one on each side, and began to beat the drum.

'One, two and three, four,
Tell me what is true,
Tell me what is true,
One and two and one and twenty,
Where in the world is old Anansi?'

They stopped and the drum gave back these words:

'One and two and one and twenty,
This will lead you to Anansi.
By the river lives a strong one;
Open him and find a rooster,
Open him and find a grain,
And within the grain, Anansi.'

At first Monkey and Tiger could not believe this. We have made a mistake, they thought. But the oracle drum said the same thing every time they tried.

'Well, let us try,' said Tiger. Down by the river they found the strong one, Mr. Alligator. They cut him open. Inside was the rooster, just as the oracle drum had said.

'Cut open the rooster,' shouted Monkey.

They cut open the rooster. There was the grain of corn, just as the oracle drum had said.

'Cut open the grain of corn,' shouted Monkey, 'and I will catch Anansi as he jumps out.'

They cut open the grain of corn, but Anansi was too quick for them. Like a flash he was off down the road. Tiger and Monkey followed fast behind him.

Again Anansi could see that they were gaining on him. As he passed a banana tree he called out, 'Banana tree, banana tree, help me.'

33

The banana tree gave Anansi one of its strong fibres. He took the fibre and quickly climbed an orange tree near by. Monkey and Tiger were catching up with him. He tied the fibre to a branch, and then he swung with the loose end to a nearby branch. To this he tied the other end, so that the fibre hung like a bridge between the two branches.

Monkey was climbing the tree. Soon he would be on the branch. Anansi climbed out to the middle of the fibre and waited.

The fibre was too weak to carry Monkey. Anansi sat out in the middle of the fibre and laughed at Monkey.

'Come, Monkey,' he mocked, 'come and catch me.'

Tiger looked up. 'Just stay there, Monkey,' he said. 'Do not move. He will soon want something to eat.'

Before long Anansi began to feel hungry. He felt hungrier than ever when Monkey said, 'Look, Tiger, you go and have your breakfast. When you come back I will go and have mine.'

Tiger came back half an hour later, smiling and licking his lips. Then Monkey went off while Tiger watched. Half an hour later Monkey came back, smiling and licking his lips. How hungry Anansi felt!

'Ah, there is a fly,' thought Anansi. 'If I go down, Tiger and Monkey will catch me. If I stay here, perhaps I can find a way of catching the fly, and that will be food enough for me.'
Slowly Anansi began to add another thread and then another to the fibre, until at last he made a web . . . and in the web was the fly.

That is why Anansi the spider lives in a web.

Anansi and the Crabs

One day Anansi took it into his head that he would like to go preaching. But he could not find anyone who would listen to him. The animals had their own preachers; the crows had a preaching crow and the birds had a preacher bird. No one wished to listen to Anansi.

Anansi was very sorry about this. He wanted to dress himself up in a long black gown and preach, but he could not find anyone who would listen to him. That was a pity. Reverend Crow looked fine in his long black gown. When he preached, all the other crows gathered round him and listened. Anansi wished that he could find someone who wanted him as a preacher.

Then one day Anansi heard that the crabs had no preacher. They had no church. So Anansi bought a long black preacher's gown and went off to Crab Town on Sunday morning. There was no church for the crabs, but there was a big tree which would serve as shelter. Anansi stood under the tree and began to preach. He preached and he preached, but not a crab came out to listen to him. They all stayed at home and slept. Anansi preached so long and so loud that he became hoarse. It was no use. The crabs slept on. Sadly he took off his long black gown and went back home.

Next Sunday morning Anansi set off for Crab Town again. This time he passed by Rat's house. Rat was standing at the door of his house, so Anansi stopped to say good-morning.

'And where are you going so early?' asked Rat, taking his pipe out of his mouth.

'I am going to church, Mr. Rat. Will you come with me?'

'I might as well,' said Rat. He put on his tall hat and his long-tailed coat, which he always wore when he went to church, and went off with Anansi.

Anansi told Rat how he had preached for a long, long time and very loud the Sunday before, and how no one had come to listen to him. Then he said:

'Mr. Rat, I am glad that you have come with me. When these crabs see a fine gentleman like you listening to me they will be sure to come and listen, too.'

When they reached Crab Town, Anansi and Rat went to the big tree. Rat sat down quietly while Anansi put on his new black preacher's gown and began to preach. He preached longer and louder than ever. Every now and then Rat nodded his head to show that he agreed. But not a crab came out. The crabs slept on.

'Can you understand it, Rat?' asked Anansi as they walked home together. 'You heard how long I preached, and how loud. You nodded your head again and again. What can we do to make the crabs come out?'

'I'll tell you what we will do,' said Rat. 'I think we should bring one or two other people. I will ask Crow and Bullfrog to come with us next week.'

The following Sunday all four friends set off for Crab Town. Anansi preached longer and louder than ever. Rat nodded his head so much that it nearly fell off. Crow called out 'Amen' every two minutes. Bullfrog gurgled 'Hallelujah.' It was a wonderful service, but no crabs came to listen. They just stayed at home and slept.

On the way back all four were silent, until Crow said, 'I wonder if they would like it better if we had some music?'

'I am sure that you are right,' said Rat. 'You bring your fiddle, Crow; and I will bring my big drums, and Bullfrog will bring his trumpet.'

Sunday came, and the friends set out once more for Crab Town with their instruments. They took their places under the big tree, and started to play.

The crabs heard the music and wondered what was happening. They sent a young crab to find out. The young crab saw Rat banging away at his big drums, 'boom, boom, boom.' John Crow fiddled away as fast as he could, so that his fiddle went 'squea, squea, squeak!' Bullfrog blew out his chest until it was twice as big as usual, and his trumpet sounded 'baw, baw, baw.' The crab listened, and then Anansi began to preach. The music seemed to be finished, so the young crab went back to his home and told the others what he had seen and heard. The crabs went back to sleep.

Anansi saw that he would have to do something still better. He asked his friends if they would allow him to baptize them in the river, and they agreed. On the following Sunday they all put on long white gowns and went to Crab Town. They marched in line, singing loudly. Rat sang tenor, while Crow and Bullfrog sang a deep loud bass. Anansi led the way to the river, and he dipped them each three times in the water – first Rat, then Crow, then Bullfrog!

When the crabs saw the baptizing they wanted to join in the fun. They hurried along to the river. 'Anansi! Anansi!' they cried. 'We want to be baptized.'

43

This was what Anansi and Rat and Crow and Bullfrog were all waiting for. 'Go put on your long white robes and come back,' they said. 'Then we'll baptize you.'

Back came the crabs in their long white gowns. Down to the river they went, four by four. Anansi, Rat, Crow and Bullfrog took the crabs and dipped them into the river – once, twice, and three times; and then they clapped them into the big sack they had handy to take them home for dinner, for they were all very fond of crab. When the bag was full, Anansi called out, 'That's all the baptizing for today,' and he and his friends started off home.

'What wonderful preaching,' said Anansi. 'We'll go back next Sunday and preach some more.'

Now on Monday morning the great King of the Crabs heard how Anansi had taken the crabs away by a trick, and he went to see his friend Alligator and made a complaint against Anansi. Alligator agreed that Anansi had no right to take crabs that way, and he promised to tell Anansi that it must never happen again. So Crab King went back to his home, and Alligator sent a message to Anansi that he wished to see him.

45

Anansi was afraid of Alligator. He was strong, and had long sharp teeth, and was not a person to trifle with. Anansi knew he had to go, so he put on a long face and went to Alligator's home by the river as fast as he could.

'Good morning, Cousin Alligator,' he said. 'How are you today?'

'What do you mean, "Cousin"?' asked Alligator. 'I didn't know you were my cousin.'

'Oh, yes,' said Anansi, 'your father and my mother were first cousins. Didn't you know that? My mother used to say, "You never need fear Alligator, because he's your cousin."'

Alligator thought about this. 'Well,' he said, 'all of us alligators can drink boiling water. If you're my cousin, you've got to prove it by drinking boiling water.'

'That I shall do, Cousin Alligator,' said Anansi. 'Pour out the water for me to drink, and I'll prove it to you.'

Alligator poured some boiling water out of the kettle into a pan and gave the pan to Anansi. Anansi lifted the pan to his mouth and pretended to drink it. 'This water isn't hot enough,' he said. 'I'll put it out in the sun to make it hotter.'

47

Alligator thought that was a good idea. So Anansi sat the pan in the sun until it had cooled off, and then he drank it.

'Now you see, I've drunk the boiling water, Cousin Alligator.'

'So you have. So you have. And I never knew we were cousins. Well, I'll keep my promise not to trouble you.'

So Anansi went home. But he didn't do any more preaching.